D0852421

For
G, B,
and P

Text and illustrations © 2010 by Alison Murray

First published under the title Apple Pie ABC in Great Britian in 2010 by Orchard Books, an imprint of Hachette Children's Books.

All rights reserved. Published by Disney • Hyperion Books, an imprint of Disney Book Group. No part of this book may be reproduced or transmitted in any form or by any means, electronic or mechanical, including photocopying, recording, or by any information storage and retrieval system, without written permission from the publisher. For information address Disney • Hyperion Books, 114 Fifth Avenue, New York, New York 10011-5690.

First U.S. edition, 2011
10 9 8 7 6 5 4 3 2 1
Printed in China
R969-8180-0-10032
Reinforced binding
ISBN 978-1-4231-3694-1
Library of Congress Cataloging-in-Publication Data on file.
Visit:
www.hyperionbooksforchildren.com

Apple Pie
ABC

Alison Murray

Disney • HYPERION BOOKS
NEW YORK

A

apple pie

B

bake it

C

cool it

D

dish it out

eager for it

F

find a crumb of it

G

get a taste
for it

have to
get a
lick of it

in trouble

J

jump up
for it

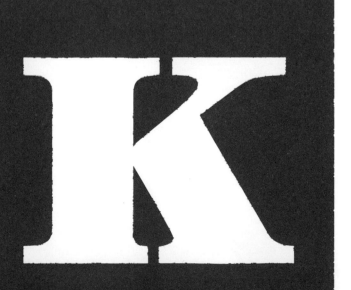

**kept away
from it**

leave
without it

miserable

N

not giving up

O

ogle it

P

pine
for it

quietly
determined

R ready

S steady

T time to go for it

U

underneath it

V

very
nearly . . .

W

whoops!

exit quickly

yum yum!

Y

z z z z z z z

**go to sleep
and dream of it**

spice

A

Sug